J
811.008   Snuffles and snouts
~~SNU~~ ROB

✓ DATE DUE

DEMCO, INC. 38-2971

DEMCO

SNUFFLES

AND

SNOUTS

Plunge into poetry

POEMS SELECTED BY **LAURA ROBB**

PICTURES BY **STEVEN KELLOGG**

Dial Books for Young Readers *New York*

For my father and mother, with love

L.R.

This book, like the very first one, is for dearest Melanie

With love

S. K.

• •

*Special thanks to Nancy Larrick for
allowing me to spend many hours in her library searching for poems.
Thanks, as well, to my husband, Lloyd, whose infinite support
and patience made this book possible.* L. R.

• •

Published by Dial Books for Young Readers
A Division of Penguin Books USA Inc.
375 Hudson Street
New York, New York 10014

Designed by Jane Byers Bierhorst
Printed in the U.S.A.
First Edition
1 3 5 7 9 10 8 6 4 2

Library of Congress Cataloging in Publication Data

Snuffles and snouts / poems selected by Laura Robb
pictures by Steven Kellogg.
p. cm.
ISBN 0-8037-1597-8. / ISBN 0-8037-1598-6 (lib. bdg.)
1. Swine—Juvenile poetry.
2. Children's poetry, American. 3. Children's poetry, English.
[1. Pigs—Poetry. 2. American poetry—Collections. 3. English poetry—Collections.]
I. Robb, Laura. II. Kellogg, Steven, ill.
PS595.S96S68 1995 811.008′036—dc20 94-9209 CIP AC

*The full-color artwork was prepared using ink and pencil line
and watercolor washes. It was then color-separated and
reproduced as red, blue, yellow, and black halftones.*

A long-tailed pig, or a short-tailed pig,
    Or a pig without e'er a tail,
A sow-pig, or a boar-pig,
    Or a pig with a curly tail.

TABLE OF

CONTENTS

Madame Froufrou's Pet Boutique

There's a pink Pig in the sitting room
Of Madame Froufrou's Pet Boutique,
Lying, oh politely, at his master's feet,
Unaware his pigpen odors
Make the customers retreat.

"Remove the Pig—that grinning creature!"
Madame Froufrou screams and shouts,
"We only clothe the best of breeds
Not pigs with broad, ringed snouts."

The Pig, by nature gentle, first grunts
Then oinks and squeals, "I have to disobey,
For my appetite increases
As each insult flies my way."

Pig gobbles up the coffee pot
Croissants, biscuits, and butter.
For salad, three geranium plants
His main course, the hair cutter.

"Farewell, begone, depart at once!"
The Pig ignores these words,
He gulps down bows and ribbons
And two unsuspecting birds.

There's a large Hog in the sitting room
Of Madame Froufrou's Pet Boutique,
Covering from wall to wall, the empty wooden floor,
Fearful his enormous size
Won't let him through the door.

Laura Robb

If Pigs Could Fly

If pigs could fly, I'd fly a pig
To foreign countries small and big—
    To Italy and Spain,
To Austria, where cowbells ring,
To Germany, where people sing—
    And then come home again.

I'd see the Ganges and the Nile;
I'd visit Madagascar's isle,
    And Persia and Peru.
People would say they'd never seen
So odd, so strange an air-machine
    As that on which I flew.

Why, everyone would raise a shout
To see his trotters and his snout
    Come floating from the sky;
And I would be a famous star
Well known in countries near and far—
    If only pigs could fly!

James Reeves

A *Drift* of Hogs

What's drifting ashore?

Not seaweed, not shells,
Not buoys, not bells,
Not notes in a bottle
Or ducks that can waddle—
It's hogs!

How did they get in the sea?

Some say they were in a canoe
When it tilted and sent them askew.
Some say they were surfing. Some say
They were fishing and floated away.

I say it's unclear,
But they're here—

All bellies and snouts and all squeals,
They certainly couldn't be seals;
Not dolphins, not dogs,
Not fishes, not frogs,

But they sun and they shift—
Look out, they're adrift!
It's hogs!

Patricia Hooper

There Once Was a Pig

There once was a pig
And she wore a wig
With golden ringlets hanging down
And all the pigs
Said, "Piggy Wig,
You're the prettiest pig in Parkertown,
    The perkiest pig
    The porkiest pig
    The pinkiest pig in Parkertown."

And all the hogs
Waddled out of their bogs
To see this pig of great renown
Saying, "Sister Sow,
We do allow
You're the prettiest pig in Parkertown.
    The plumpiest pig
    The pluckiest pig
    The pinkiest pig in Parkertown."

Then all the pigs
Put on big wigs
With golden ringlets hanging down
And danced jig jogs
With all the hogs
They danced all over Parkertown.
Danced jiggety jigs
Danced joggety jogs
The pigs and the hogs of Parkertown.

Mary Ann Hoberman

The Piguana

Snout too little
Tail too big,
Still it looks
A lot like pig.

Serve it hot
With wine or root,
Still it tastes
A lot like newt.

Jane Yolen

Why Pigs Cannot Write Poems

Pigs cannot write poems because
Nothing rhymes with *oink*. If you
Think you can find a rhyme, I'll pause,
But if I wait until you do,
I'll have forgotten why it was
Pigs cannot write poems because.

John Ciardi

Piglet Perfume

She pokes her shiny, flat pink snout
out through the wooden farmyard fence
and nuzzles, slobbers on my hand.
I tell my mother I can't wash.
I need to keep the smell all day—
the smell of piglet, barn, and hay.

Ann Whitford Paul

How to View a Pig

Look at a pig from the front, no doubt,
Every time you'll see his snout.

It's round and pink, and not too clean
Unlike most noses you have seen!

Now turn the pig half way about,
It's difficult to see his snout.

However, then you cannot fail
To see a pig's curly tail.

Lloyd Robb

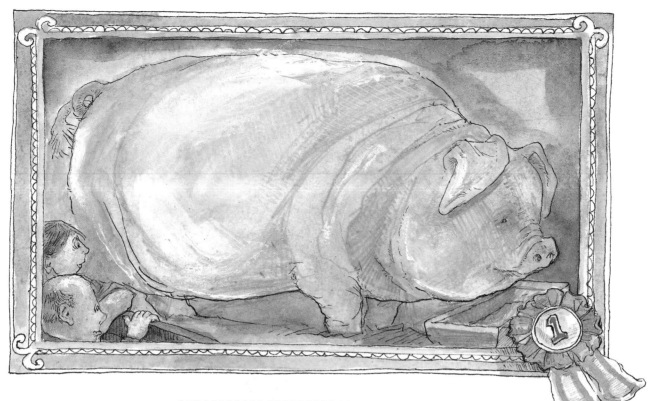

Prize Winner: State Fair

squinting eye to eye
at the gawkers leaning on
the rails of his pen . . .

hunkering over
his dish of mash, ignoring
his bright blue ribbon . . .

shining and gleaming
like a huge heavy chunk of
polished pink marble . . .

Myra Cohn Livingston

17

The Pig-Tale

There was a Pig that sat alone
     Beside a ruined Pump:
By day and night he made his moan—
It would have stirred a heart of stone
To see him wring his hoofs and groan,
     Because he could not jump.

There was a Frog that wandered by—
     A sleek and shining lump:
Inspected him with fishy eye,
And said, "O Pig, what makes you cry?"
And bitter was that Pig's reply,
     "Because I cannot jump!"

That Frog he grinned a grin of glee,
    And hit his chest a thump.
"O Pig," he said, "be ruled by me,
And you shall see what you shall see.
This minute, for a trifling fee,
    I'll teach you how to jump!

"You may be faint from many a fall,
    And bruised by many a bump:
But, if you persevere through all,
And practice first on something small,
Concluding with a ten-foot wall,
    You'll find that you *can* jump!"

That Pig looked up with joyful start:
    "O Frog, you *are* a trump!
Your words have healed my inward smart—
Come, name your fee and do your part:
Bring comfort to a broken heart,
    By teaching me to jump!"

"My fee shall be a mutton-chop,
  My goal this ruined Pump.
Observe with what an airy flop
I plant myself upon the top!
Now bend your knees and take a hop,
  For that's the way to jump!"

Uprose that Pig, and rushed, full whack,
     Against the ruined Pump:
Rolled over like an empty sack,
And settled down upon his back,
While all his bones at once went "Crack!"
     It was a fatal jump.

That Pig lay still as any stone,
    And could not stir a stump:
Nor ever, if the truth were known,
Was he again observed to moan,
Nor ever wring his hoofs and groan,
    Because he could not jump.

MABEL
PERISHED
ON TUESDAY

BECAUSE
HE
COULD NOT JUMP

AL.
SQUISHED

That Frog made no remark, for he
    Was dismal as a dump:
He knew the consequence must be
That he would never get his fee—
And still he sits, in miserie,
    Upon that ruined Pump!

Lewis Carroll

The Pig

The pig is not a nervous beast;
He never worries in the least.
He lives his tranquil life unshaken,
And when he dies brings home the bacon.

Roland Young

Paddy Pork

Paddy Pork
   wakes at nine,
     steps across
       the other swine.

Trots to market,
   buys an ax,
     lugs it home
       in paper sacks.

Paddy heaves-
   Ho—high!
     Heavens, how
       the chips fly!

Piggies, hens,
   & roosters stop,
     watching Paddy
       Pork chop.

J. Patrick Lewis

Three Little Pigs

Oh, the farmer had one,
And the farmer had two,
And the farmer had three
Little pigs in a stew,
    Tra-la-la.

They were wrapped up in batter,
They were wrapped up in dough,
They were stewed, they were spiced,
They were baked, O-ho!
    Tra-la-la.

When the piglets were finished,
The farmer looked in.
But he never could eat them
For fear 'twas a sin.
    Tra-la-la.

Oh, the pigs sang a carol,
The farmer joined in,
With the eating forgotten
Amidst all the din,
    Tra-la-la.

Traditional : American

The Pigs

Piggie Wig and Piggie Wee,
Hungry pigs as pigs could be,
For their dinner had to wait
Down behind the barnyard gate.

Piggie Wig and Piggie Wee
Climbed the barnyard gate to see,
Peeping through the gate so high,
But no dinner could they spy.

Piggie Wig and Piggie Wee
Got down sad as pigs could be;
But the gate soon opened wide
And they scampered forth outside.

Piggie Wig and Piggie Wee,
What was their delight to see?
Dinner ready not far off—
Such a full and tempting trough!

Piggie Wig and Piggie Wee,
Greedy pigs as pigs could be,
For their dinner ran pell-mell;
In the trough both piggies fell.

Emilie Poulsson

A Pig Tale

Poor Jane Higgins,
She had five piggins,
And one got drowned in the Irish Sea.
Poor Jane Higgins,
She had four piggins,
And one flew over a sycamore tree.
Poor Jane Higgins,
She had three piggins,
And one was taken away for pork.
Poor Jane Higgins,
She had two piggins,
And one was sent to the Bishop of Cork.
Poor Jane Higgins,
She had one piggin,
And that was struck by a shower of hail,
So poor Jane Higgins,
She had no piggins,
And that's the end of my little pig tale.

James Reeves

Genetics

I bought a blue pig, called her Sue,
Then a yellow one, called him Lou.
I kept and fed them in a sty,
Above the ground, below the sky.
    Soon four piglets could be seen,
    One blue, one yellow, and two green.

Lloyd Robb

A Pig Is Never Blamed

A pig is never blamed in case
he forgets to wash his face.
No dirty suds are on his soap,
because with soap he does not cope.
He never has to clean the tub
after he has had a scrub,
for whatever mess he makes,
a bath is what he never takes.
But then, what is a pool to him?
Poor pig, he never learns to swim.
And all the goodies he can cram
down his gullet turn to ham.
It's mean:
keeping clean.
You hardly want to, till you're very big.
But it's worse to be a pig.

Babette Deutsch

The Hog

Some scientist may at last disperse
The mysteries of the universe,
But me, I cannot even think
Why pork is white and ham is pink.

Ogden Nash

Pig Nap

One step . . . another . . .
Sinking down,
she wallows in
the mud wet ground,
rolls lazy over,
settles deep,
blissful in
the squishy seep
and ooze of slime.
Pig dozes in
a quilt of grime.

Ann Whitford Paul

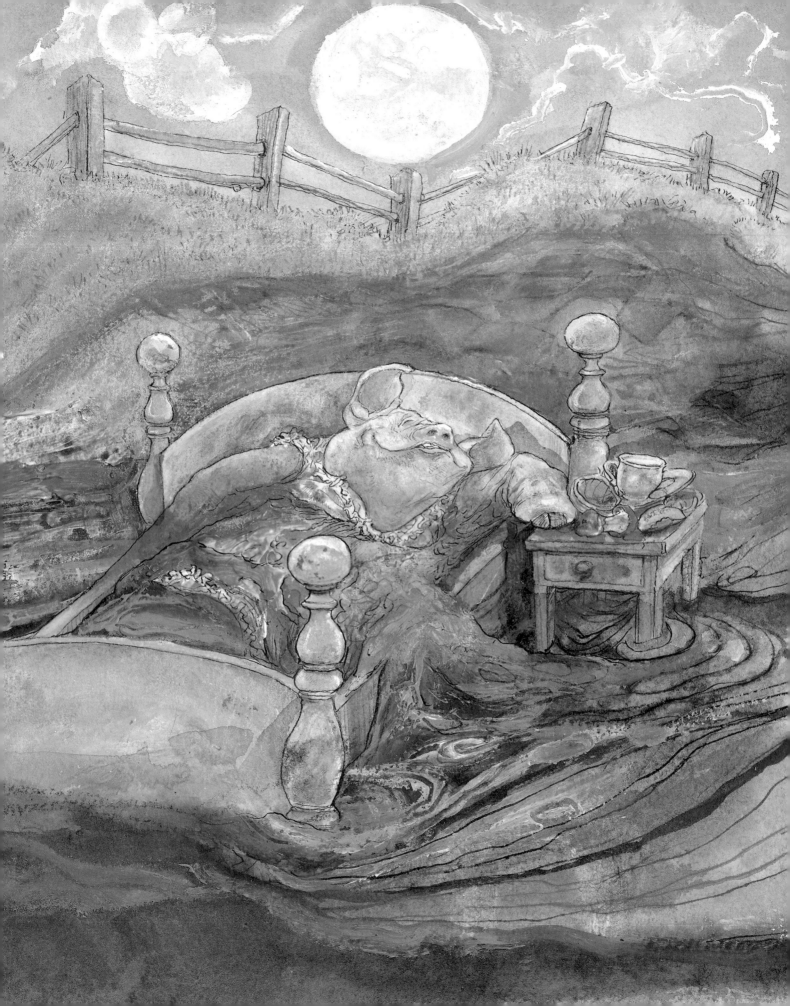

Pig-Sty

O my!
Sit-in-the-sty,
Why do you snivel and sniff and cry?
I've married a Swineherd without any feelings
But for turnip-parings and apple-peelings.

Fie, fie,
Sit-in-the-sty!
Blow your nose and wipe your eye,
Scratch the old sow and make the best of it,
Peelings and parings and all the rest of it!

Eleanor Farjeon

The Lady and the Swine

There was a lady loved a swine;
    "Honey," said she,
"Pig-hog, wilt thou be mine?"
    "Oink," said he.

"I'll build for thee a silver sty,
    Honey," said she,
"And in it softly thou shalt lie."
    "Oink," said he.

"Pinned with a silver pin,
    Honey," said she,
"That you may go both out and in."
    "Oink," said he.

"When shall we two be wed,
    Honey?" said she.
"Oink, oink, oink," he said,
    And away went he.

English Folk Rhyme

The Pigs and the Charcoal-Burner

The old Pig said to the little pigs,
    "In the forest is truffles and mast,
Follow me then, all ye little pigs,
    Follow me fast!"

The Charcoal-burner sat in the shade
    With his chin on his thumb,
And saw the big Pig and the little pigs
    Chuffling come.

He watched 'neath a green and giant bough,
    And the pigs in the ground
Made a wonderful grizzling and gruzzling
    And a greedy sound.

And when, full-fed they were gone, and Night
    Walked her starry ways,
He stared with his cheeks in his hands
    At his sullen blaze.

Walter de la Mare

Summertime

Was ever a pig
contented as this,
to roll in the mud
and know the bliss
of cooling off
in the muck
and grime,
having the grubbiest
mussiest
time?

and then, when he's cool,
to slowly rise
and dry himself off
in the summer skies,
and sniff for his supper
and slop up his feed—
What else does a
does a happy
piggy
need?

Myra Cohn Livingston

A Little Pig Asleep

Behind Devaney's barn I saw
A little pig asleep.
His eyes were squiggened up so tight,
I'm sure he couldn't peep.

I crept right up beside him
And peeked 'way down his ear.
I'll bet he never even dreamed
A little boy was near.

His skin was full of bristles
From his forehead to his toes.
He had shellac on all his feet
And rubber on his nose.

Leroy F. Jackson

The Prayer of the Little Pig

Lord,
   their politeness makes me laugh!
   Yes, I grunt!
   Grunt and snuffle!
   I grunt because I grunt
   and snuffle
   because I cannot do anything else!
   All the same, I am not going to thank them
   for fattening me up to make bacon.
   Why did You make me so tender?
   What a fate!
   Lord,
   teach me how to say

      Amen.

Carmen Bernos De Gasztold

Acknowledgments

Introductory poem taken from Marguerite de Angeli's *Book of Nursery and Mother Goose Rhymes*, Doubleday & Company, 1954 / *Madame Froufrou's Pet Boutique* Copyright © 1995 by Laura Robb / *If Pigs Could Fly* from *Collected Children's Poems of James Reeves*. Reprinted by permission of The Estate of James Reeves / *A Drift of Hogs* from *A Bundle of Beasts* by Patricia Hooper. Text copyright © 1987 by Patricia Hooper. Reprinted by permission of Houghton Mifflin Co. All rights reserved / *There Once Was a Pig* Reprinted by permission of Gina Maccoby Literary Agency. Copyright © 1981 by Mary Ann Hoberman / *The Piguana* Reprinted by permission of Curtis Brown, Ltd. Copyright © 1980 by Jane Yolen / *Why Pigs Cannot Write Poems* from *Doodle Soup* by John Ciardi. Text copyright © 1985 by Myra J. Ciardi. Reprinted by permission of Houghton Mifflin Co. All rights reserved / *Piglet Perfume* Copyright © 1995 by Ann Whitford Paul / *How to View a Pig* Copyright © 1995 by Lloyd Robb / *Prize Winner: State Fair* Copyright © 1995 by Myra Cohn Livingston. Used by permission of Marian Reiner for the author / Excerpts from *The Pig-Tale* taken from *Sylvie and Bruno* by Lewis Carroll, first published in 1889 / *Paddy Pork* from *Ridicholas Nicholas: More Animal Poems* by J. Patrick Lewis. Copyright © 1995 by J. Patrick Lewis. Used by permission of Dial Books for Young Readers, a division of Penguin Books USA Inc / *A Pig Tale* Reprinted by permission of The Estate of James Reeves from *The Collected Children's Poems of James Reeves* / *Genetics* Copyright © 1995 by Lloyd Robb / *A Pig Is Never Blamed* from *The Random House Book of Poetry for Children*. Copyright © 1983 by Babette Deutsch. Reprinted by permission of Adam Yarmolinsky for the author / *The Hog* from *The Old Dog Barks Backwards* by Ogden Nash. Copyright © 1968 and 1971 by Ogden Nash. Reprinted by permission of Little, Brown and Company and Curtis Brown, Ltd. / *Pig Nap* Copyright © 1995 by Ann Whitford Paul / *Pig-Sty* Reprinted by permission of Harold Ober Associates Incorporated. Copyright © 1942 by Eleanor Farjeon / *The Pigs and the Charcoal-Burner* Reprinted by permission of The Literary Trustees of Walter de la Mare and the Society of Authors as their representative / *Summertime* Copyright © 1995 by Myra Cohn Livingston. Used by permission of Marian Reiner for the author / *A Little Pig Asleep* by Leroy F. Jackson. Copyright © 1932 by Child Life, Inc. Permission granted by Ruth W. Jackson, daughter-in-law of author / *The Prayer of the Little Pig* from *Prayers from the Ark* by Carmen Bernos De Gasztold, illustrated by Jean Primrose, translated by Rumer Godden. Translation copyright © 1962 by Rumer Godden. Original copyright © 1947, © 1955 by Editions du Cloitre. Used by permission of Viking Penguin, a division of Penguin Books USA Inc.